MY SCHOOL, YOUR SCHOOL, OUR SCHOOLS

by EMMA CARLSON BERNE
Illustrations by MICAH PLAYER
Music by MARK MALLMAN

CANTATA
LEARNING

WWW.CANTATALEARNING.COM

Published by Cantata Learning
1710 Roe Crest Drive
North Mankato, MN 56003
www.cantatalearning.com

Library of Congress Cataloging-in-Publication Data
Names: Berne, Emma Carlson, author. | Player, Micah, illustrator. | Mallman, Mark, composer.
Title: My school, your school, our schools / by Emma Carlson Berne ; illustrations by Micah Player ; music by Mark Mallman.
Description: North Mankato, MN : Cantata Learning, 2019. | Series: How we are alike and different | Audience: K to grade 3.
Identifiers: LCCN 2017056297 (print) | LCCN 2017058409 (ebook) | ISBN 9781684102679 (eBook) | ISBN 9781684102419 (hardcover : alk. paper) | ISBN 9781684102938 (paperback : alk. paper)
Subjects: LCSH: Schools--Cross-cultural studies--Juvenile literature.
Classification: LCC LB1556 (ebook) | LCC LB1556 .B47 2019 (print) | DDC 371--dc23
LC record available at https://lccn.loc.gov/2017056297

Book design and art direction, Tim Palin Creative
Editorial direction, Kellie M. Hultgren
Music direction, Elizabeth Draper
Music arranged and produced by Mark Mallman

TIPS TO SUPPORT LITERACY AT HOME

WHY READING AND SINGING WITH YOUR CHILD IS SO IMPORTANT

Daily reading with your child leads to increased academic achievement. Music and songs, specifically rhyming songs, are a fun and easy way to build early literacy and language development. Music skills correlate significantly with both phonological awareness and reading development. Singing helps build vocabulary and speech development. And reading and appreciating music together is a wonderful way to strengthen your relationship.

READ AND SING EVERY DAY!

TIPS FOR USING CANTATA LEARNING BOOKS AND SONGS DURING YOUR DAILY STORY TIME

1. As you sing and read, point out the different words on the page that rhyme. Suggest other words that rhyme.
2. Memorize simple rhymes such as Itsy Bitsy Spider and sing them together. This encourages comprehension skills and early literacy skills.
3. Use the questions in the back of each book to guide your singing and storytelling.
4. Read the included sheet music with your child while you listen to the song. How do the music notes correlate to the words of the song?
5. Sing along on the go and at home. Access music by scanning the QR code on each Cantata book. You can also stream or download the music for free to your computer, smartphone, or mobile device.

Devoting time to daily reading shows that you are available for your child. Together, you are building language, literacy, and listening skills.

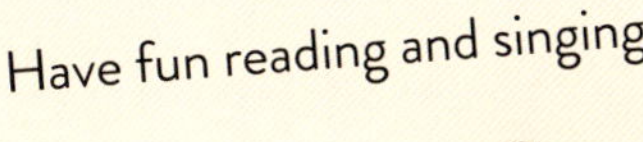

Have fun reading and singing!

Learning is part of growing up, and school is part of learning. Almost everywhere in the world, children go to some kind of school. They might go to a big school in a city or a tiny school in the mountains, or they might have school at home. But no matter where children go to school, they **study** hard and learn.

Let's sing together about school around the world!

BUS STOP

My school has a lot of rooms,
a **teacher** in each one.

It has a playground outside, too,
where we can swing and run.

Aa Bb Cc Dd Ee Ff Gg Hh Ii Jj Kk
NOUN
VERB

Schools are different all over the land,
but teachers are here with a helping hand.

Learning slow or learning fast,
on a desk or on the grass,
with lots of kids or just a few,
we study hard and learn at school.

My school, it has just one room.
One teacher helps us all.

All day long, each grade works hard,
all children, big and small.

Schools are different all over the land,
but teachers are here with a helping hand.

Learning slow or learning fast,
on a desk or on the grass,
with lots of kids or just a few,
we study hard and learn at school.

My school comes to me at home,
here on this kitchen stool.

My friend lives at school all week.
She goes to **boarding school**.

Schools are different all over the land,
but teachers are here with a helping hand.

Learning slow or learning fast,
on a desk or on the grass,
with lots of kids or just a few,
we study hard and learn at school.

Our school has no walls at all.
We sit under the trees.

We share our books there in the shade.
Our desks are on our knees.

Schools are different all over the land,
but teachers are here with a helping hand.

Learning slow or learning fast,
on a desk or on the grass,
with lots of kids or just a few,
we study hard and learn at school.

SONG LYRICS

My School, Your School, Our Schools

My school has a lot of rooms,
a teacher in each one.

It has a playground outside, too,
where we can swing and run.

Schools are different all over the land,
but teachers are here with a helping hand.

Learning slow or learning fast,
on a desk or on the grass,
with lots of kids or just a few,
we study hard and learn at school.

My school, it has just one room.
One teacher helps us all.

All day long, each grade works hard,
all children, big and small.

Schools are different all over the land,
but teachers are here with a helping hand.

Learning slow or learning fast,
on a desk or on the grass,
with lots of kids or just a few,
we study hard and learn at school.

My school comes to me at home,
here on this kitchen stool.

My friend lives at school all week.
She goes to boarding school.

Schools are different all over the land,
but teachers are here with a helping hand.

Learning slow or learning fast,
on a desk or on the grass,
with lots of kids or just a few,
we study hard and learn at school.

Our school has no walls at all.
We sit under the trees.

We share our books there in the shade.
Our desks are on our knees.

Schools are different all over the land,
but teachers are here with a helping hand.

Learning slow or learning fast,
on a desk or on the grass,
with lots of kids or just a few,
we study hard and learn at school.

My School, Your School, Our Schools

Pop
Mark Mallman

Verse 2
My school, it has just one room.
One teacher helps us all.
All day long, each grade works hard,
all children, big and small.

Chorus

Verse 3
My school comes to me at home,
here on this kitchen stool.
My friend lives at school all week.
She goes to boarding school.

Chorus

Verse 4
Our school has no walls at all.
We sit under the trees.
We share our books there in the shade.
Our desks are on our knees.

Chorus

GLOSSARY

boarding school—a school at which children live

study—read, write, and listen to a teacher to learn

teacher—a person who helps others to learn

CRITICAL THINKING QUESTIONS

1. Name two kinds of schools this song describes. How are these schools different? How are they the same?
2. What is your own school like? Describe it! Draw a map to show where you sit, where you do your favorite activity, and where you eat lunch.
3. Would you like to try going to a different kind of school? Which kind of school would you be curious to try?

TO LEARN MORE

Falk, Laine. *This Is the Way We Go to School.* New York: Scholastic, 2009.

Ruurs, Margriet. *School Days Around the World.* Toronto, ON: Kids Can Press, 2015.

Smith, Penny, and Zahavit Shalev. *A School Like Mine: A Celebration of Schools Around the World.* New York: DK, 2016.